LOUD

By Katy S. Duffield

Pictures by Mike Boldt

two lions

By

two lions

Text copyright © 2015 by Katy S. Duffield
Illustrations copyright © 2015 by Mike Boldt
All rights reserved.

No part of this book may be reproduced, or stored in a retrieval system, or transmitted in any form or by any means, electronic, mechanical, photocopying, recording, or otherwise, without express written permission of the publisher.

Published by Two Lions, New York

www.apub.com

Amazon, the Amazon logo, and Two Lions are trademarks of Amazon.com, Inc., or its affiliates.

ISBN-13: 9781477827765 (hardcover)
ISBN-10: 1477827765 (Hardcover)
ISBN-13: 9781477827857 (paperback)
ISBN-10: 1477827854 (paperback)

The illustrations are rendered in digital media.
Book design by Jennifer Browning

Printed in China
First Edition

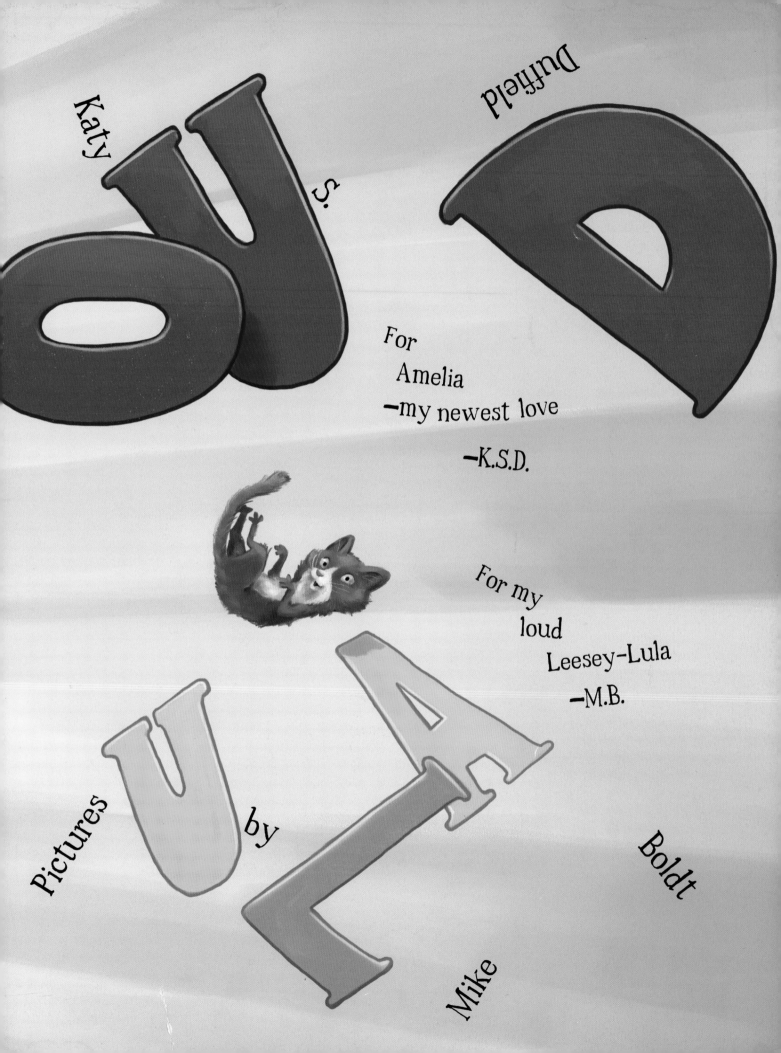

LOUD

Katy S. Duffield

For
Amelia
—my newest love
—K.S.D.

For my
loud
Leesey–Lula
—M.B.

Pictures by

Mike Boldt

Lula was born smack-dab in the middle of one of the biggest twisters Pryor County had ever seen. Winds howled. Trees snapped.

...it wasn't as loud as Lula.

When Doc Clements delivered Lula
and she let out her first cry—

—that ol' storm sounded like nothing more than a chicken feather hitting the henhouse floor.

Lula spent her growing years like most young'uns–'cept A LOT louder.

When she called her kitten for supper, every cat all the way from Crowley's Corner came a-callin'.

HERE KITTY

And Lula wreaked ten kinds of havoc when she moseyed into the public library.

Got any books That'll Turn over my Tickle Box?

READ

Librarian

In the fall of her fifth year, Lula's pa said to Lula's ma, "What are we gonna do about our Loud Lula?"

"Don't know," said Ma, "but hollering won't be welcome at the schoolhouse."

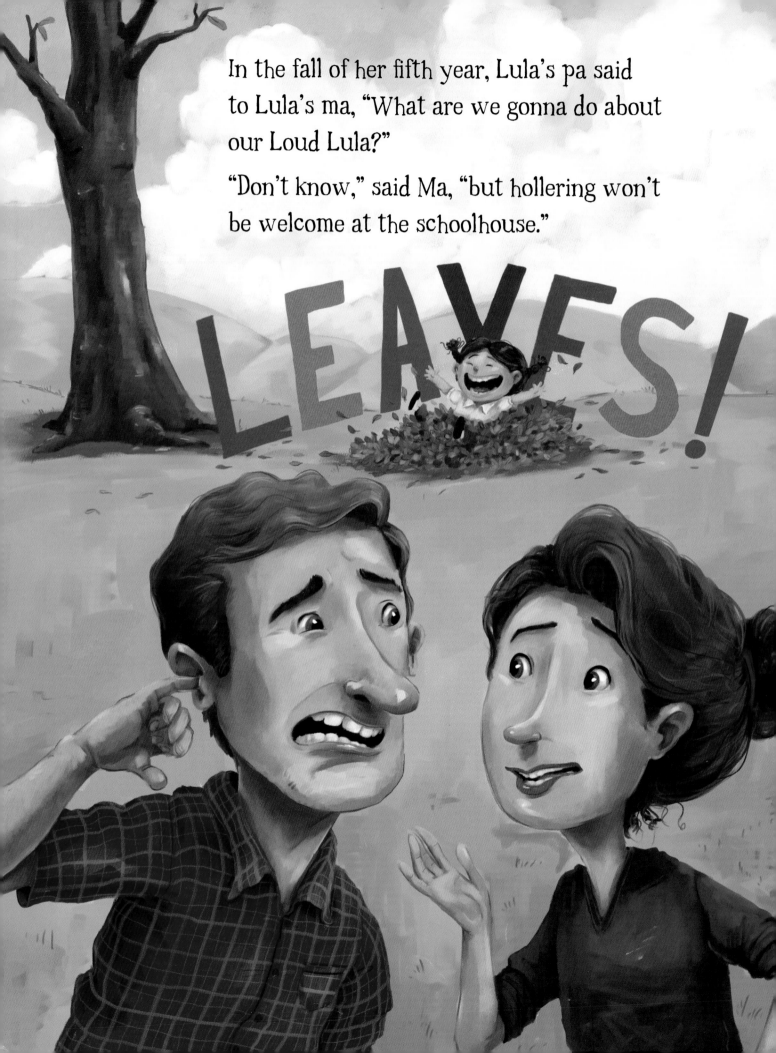

LEAVES!

Ma and Pa walked Lula to school on the first day.

"We love you," said Ma.

"Be good," said Pa. But he really wanted to say

"BE QUIET!"

BYE, MA!
BYE, PA!

Lula's teacher welcomed her students.

"Howdy-do, Miss Idabelle," said Jenny Sue.

"When's recess?" asked Joe Bob.

Then Lula raised her hand.

Lula's earsplitting question had the whole schoolhouse
shakin' like a big ol' bowl of boysenberry jelly.

When the dust settled, Miss Idabelle said, "Lula, in the schoolhouse, we need to use our inside voices."

During math, Jenny Sue began counting. "One."

Joe Bob followed with "Two."

Then it was Lula's turn:

THREE!!!

Lula's earth-shattering shout sloshed every last speck of water out of the fishbowl.

Slither, the class snake, jiggled right out of his skin.

"Lula!" Miss Idabelle began. "*PLEASE* remember to use your . . ."

"*. . . INSIDE VOICE!*"
the kids cried.

That afternoon, Miss Idabelle was plumb tuckered out. "Let's have a short quiet time."

The other students were tuckered out, too. But not Lula. She felt as spry as a spring chicken.

Suddenly, Lula caught sight of
something outside the window.

It grew bigger and
bigger

as it moved closer and
closer.

Lula had to tell someone! And
for the first time, she wondered,

Reckon I ought to use my *INSIDE* voice?

So she did.
Lula hollered in her inside voice
(which wasn't too different from
her outside voice)—

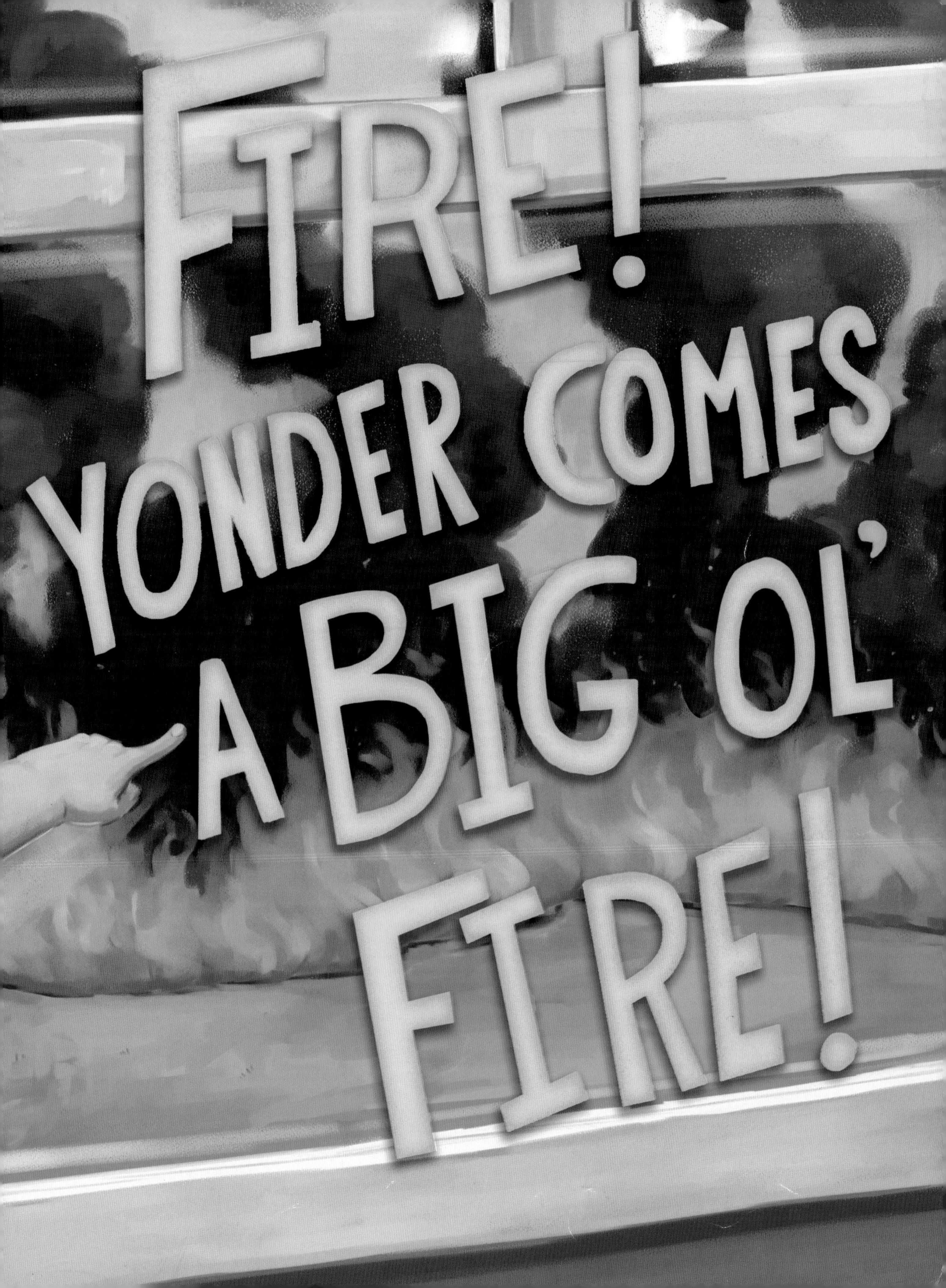
FIRE!
YONDER COMES
A BIG OL'
FIRE!

Lula's voice romped through the town, echoed in the hills, and stretched its loudness across five counties— alerting a heap of fire trucks.

The way some folks tell it, those firefighters didn't even have to pull out their hoses. Lula's rip-roaring holler ran that wildfire back across the hills!

yar County Gazette

GRANNY SHELBY'S PEACH COBBLER, P. 7

PUPPIES, P. 23

LITTLE GAL WITH A
SAVES

Though some p
difficult to bel
5, saved Pryor
devastation o

Lula alerted folk
wildfire was he
voice summon
state. But it w
that stopped
"I ain't ever
Captain A
that fire.
ears are
have h

"I just used my inside voice."

P
R

LONG-TIME TEACHER PLANS
RETIREMENT
...acher Miss Idabelle reports that
...d of the school year.

From that day on, Lula became more famous than Granny Shelby's finger-lickin' peach cobbler, more famous even than ol' Wally Hubbard's coon dog and her twenty-three puppies.

And no one ever complained about Lula's hollering again.

' OL' VOICE OWN

find it
Lula Jordan,
nty from major
day.

BIG way!) that a raging
ward town. Lula's loud
ighters from across the
e firefighters' actions
ze; it was Lula herself.
nything like it," said Fire
n. "Her hollering spooked
a way, I can understand; my
ging. If I'd had a choice, I'd
he other way, too!"

**COUNTY LIBRARY TO BE
VATED**

deling plans are in the works for
ryor County Library. The library had
ined damages over the years, thanks to a
y boisterous resident," as librarian Luke
informed the Gazette. Plans for the
avier desks, chairs, globes,

Well, not too often, anyway.

Louder!

DEXTER DINO,
SOAR THROUGH
THE SKY.
DEXTER DINO,
WAY UP
HIGH!

Look, Jack, we're flying!

Hey! Guess what?

After the nice lady asked us to stop singing so loudly, she showed us how to watch a movie and gave us this supersoft, snuggly blankie.

And that's not even the best part....

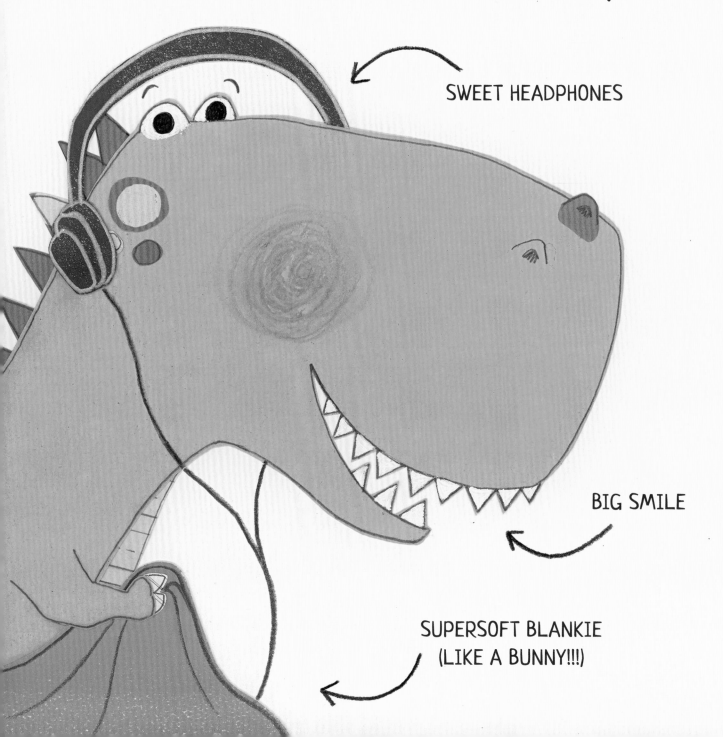

SWEET HEADPHONES

BIG SMILE

SUPERSOFT BLANKIE
(LIKE A BUNNY!!!)

LOOK AT ALL THESE COOKIES!

Jack and I **LOVE** cookies.
Maybe flying isn't so bad . . .

...especially when you have your best friend there to keep you company.

And a few extra cookies.

Look! We made it!

And you were so worried.

DEXTER DINO,
BIG AND BRAVE.
DEXTER DINO,
RIDE THAT WAVE!
greetings
FROM
FLORIDA!
THE SUNSHINE STATE